Finding My Way:
Daisy's Story

by
Kevin John Smith

Based on a true story

Thank you Jan for your constant love and support.

Dedicated to Jessica and Savannah.

Table of Contents

"The two most important days in your life are the day you are born and the day you find out why." ~ Mark Twain

"Some would say I never should've left home. There's a certain safety in that. The streets were dangerous, and I got hurt there. But I wouldn't trade any of it, because it shaped me to become who I am. I've discovered who I am and I understand my purpose." ~ Daisy

Chapter 1

On My Own in Mexico

Dear Mom,

The sound of a car horn in front of our house woke me up. You slept right through it. From under the front porch, I peeked out beyond the fence to see what was going on. I looked out at the road and couldn't believe my eyes. The gate was open! The gate was open and no one was around. Why was the gate open?

This was a chance to explore things on my own. I loved our walks outside, but we were always on the leash and we never went very far. I couldn't resist the urge. As I laid there in the cool dirt under the porch my mind raced. What would I do, where would I go? I began to imagine what was beyond the few blocks our owners had allowed us to see. In that moment, I was consumed by thoughts of what the world outside the gate was like.

I crawled on my belly through the small trench you dug for us. Standing up I looked around but saw no one. I hesitated for a moment, thinking maybe I should bark and let the owners know they left the gate open. That was our job, to alert humans to things. But this time I didn't bark, and in that moment of indecision, with my heart racing and tail wagging, I ran for the gate.

Right away things began to feel different. I was excited and a little afraid at the same time. People on the street avoided me. Some even seemed afraid of me. It felt different on the street without our owners, but I was excited! I could go wherever I wanted to, and I did. At first I wandered our usual stomping grounds, seeing all the places and people, sniffing the same garbage and peeing in the usual spots. I passed the big church on the corner, stopped briefly behind our owners favorite taco stand for a few scraps, then crossed through the town plaza where our owner would always turn around and head back. I would stop when I wanted to stop, but mostly I just kept walking. It was so much fun. I would walk a little, then run a little, then walk some more.

Then I met a new friend. I followed him to a park. I had never been to this park. It was like our park, only bigger, and with more people. We played in the grass for hours. He chased me and I chased him. He could hardly keep up with me, I had so much energy. Eventually my friend wandered over to a patch of shade under an old worn out sliding board and laid down in the cool dirt. I was so tired from my long run and playing in the park that I laid down under the same sliding board and fell asleep next to him. I was exhausted and hot.

When I awoke my friend was gone. I looked around and suddenly realized, I didn't know where I was. It was dark and nothing looked, smelled or sounded familiar. It was very loud compared to where we live. I was getting hungry. By now the owners would have brought us our dinner. I walked in the direction that I hoped was towards home. The streets were very confusing, and there were so many cars. Everything looked so different at night. All the cars had lights that shine right in your eyes making it so hard to see. I walked for hours, until I finally came across something familiar. 'I know this place,' I thought, 'I've been here before'. As I glanced around the space I realized that it was the park where I fell asleep. I had walked in a circle. Our little city was pretty quiet by this time, and I still had not eaten any dinner. The cool desert air began to set in. I felt afraid. I remembered what you said Mom, "A dog alone on the streets in Mexico is not safe".

I kept hearing those words over and over in my mind. I was no longer thinking about where I would go, or who I would meet, but rather what would I eat and where would I sleep? I cautiously made my way back to the space under the sliding board. I hoped that maybe this would be a safe place to sleep for the night. All the people had left. I laid there for the longest time, trying to sleep with one eye open. I never intended to spend the night away.

Chapter 2

The Streets of Santa Rosalia

Dear Mom,

The next morning, I awoke to a sharp pain in my lower left back. It caused me to jump up so fast that I hit my head on the bottom of the old sliding board. Before I knew what happened I felt another pain, this time just below my left ear and much harder. Turning to my left I saw a small group of boys with rocks in their hands. They were pointing at me and laughing loudly. I ran as fast as I could in the opposite direction. As I ran away I saw the rocks landing all around me. I felt a final rock glance across my back leg. I never looked back.

They were yelling, "Get out of here you mangy mutt!"

I kept running until I couldn't hear them anymore. My backside and head hurt badly from the rocks. I stood on the sidewalk outside a market and cried. I must have made too much noise, because soon after a man from the store came out with a broom swinging at me.

"Stop bothering my customers, go home where you belong," he said.

I wished I could go home. As I crossed the street I heard a loud car horn right next to me and the sound of screeching brakes. In all the excitement I forgot to look out for cars and almost got hit. I scurried to the other side of the street. I hoped to find someplace where I could rest and lick my wounds, but I had no idea where to go. I didn't feel safe going back to the park and that was the only place I knew.

I was really hungry. I drank some water from small pools on the streets. It wasn't like our water at home, but that didn't matter. I was so thirsty. I was beginning to lose hope of finding my way home. This part of town looked very different from our neighborhood. There were more people, more cars, and more dogs. There were dogs inside the fences and even more outside the fences. It was noisier here and some places smelled bad.

Most of the people didn't want me near them. The dogs were even worse. There were groups of dogs. Some of the groups were meaner than others. Many of the dogs on the street limped, some even had no tail. Some had bugs all over their faces. There were very few old dogs. Mostly young dogs that looked sad and old. The dogs inside the fences looked better than the ones on the street. Every time I passed a dog inside a fence they would bark at me until I left. I guess they were warning their owners just like you did, Mom. The dogs with owners looked well fed. The street dogs were all skinny. Some of them were so skinny you could see their ribs and other bones. I saw a couple of dogs that only had three legs.

Days went by with very little to eat. I spent most of my time searching for food and trying to stay out of the hot sun. It was not easy. Sometimes other dogs stole the things I found to eat. My days on the streets were long and hot, but it was the nights that were scariest. That's when the pack dogs ruled the streets. I've seen them abuse other dogs, especially the females. I've even seen them kill and eat weaker dogs and cats. The cats were pretty smart though. They took to the high ground at night. They travelled the city on the roof tops and patio walls. I tried to lay low at night, but stayed alert. I slept more during the day. It was safer in the daytime.

Chapter 3

Traffic

Dear Mom,

I have grown taller, but I know I am skinnier. Finding food has been hard. My short light brown hair has become dirty and dry. But that's not the worst part.

I learned how to cross the streets without getting hit by watching the other dogs. There were a couple of close calls, mostly my fault, but I survived. After several weeks I had gotten pretty good at it.

One day the wind was blowing so hard that I barely opened my eyes all day. I squinted to keep the dirt and sand out. There were very few people on the streets that day, but there were a lot more cars.

It was late afternoon. I was hungry, thirsty and tired. I spotted a puddle across the street. I looked to my left squinting into the wind and the sun. It looked clear. I checked to the right and headed towards the puddle. I don't remember everything exactly, but I remember hearing the sound of a car horn so loud it pierced my ears.

I think I froze. I never saw what hit me. It was a surreal moment where it felt like everything was moving in slow motion. Then I realized what happened. My first clue was the pain in my back left leg. I cried out! It was agonizing. All I could think of was to run. My mind was racing. I cried and cried. I ran down the street dragging one leg behind me. My leg wouldn't work! I remember thinking as I ran and cried, is this how I die? How could I get hit by a car? I knew better. The pain was unbearable and running only made it worse. After running for what seemed like forever, I curled up on the sidewalk next to a telephone pole. After all that effort, I had only ran about a half a block. I laid there and cried. I was hoping no one would hear me, because they would chase me away, but I couldn't stop crying.

The car that hit me never stopped, but I didn't expect it to. Some of the meaner dogs would bite you if you came near them, so most people stayed away from all street dogs. I watched the car drive off. Across the street I heard people laughing at me getting hit. There's not much compassion for street dogs. Many street dogs get poisoned by people who are tired of them digging in their trash.

The laughter was soon drowned out by the sound of a motorcycle. It was coming right at me. I tried to get up, but it was too painful. I closed my eyes. The motorcycle stopped right in front of me. I opened my eyes and saw Isidro starring down at me.

Isidro was a man many of the street dogs knew. He worked in the parks sweeping up and emptying the trash. Sometimes he brought bones to work and gave them to the dogs. It's a miracle that Isidro drove up when he did. He saw the whole thing from down the street. He was heading to church with a guitar strapped to his back. He often played music at the church services. Isidro, a tall slender man, drove an old red motorcycle that I often saw around town. He always drove too fast and never wore a helmet. His long black hair blowing behind him made him very recognizable around town.

Isidro hurried to park his motorcycle and began to approach me slowly. He looked a bit nervous. I slowed down my crying to a whimper.

"It's going to be ok girl, it's going to be ok," he said in a soft voice.

His words were very comforting. Until I heard those words, I thought for sure I would curl up next to that telephone poll and die. Then Isidro stooped down and scooped me up into his arms. I cried from the pain in my leg as it pressed against his chest. He left his motorcycle behind, and at a very brisk pace with me in his arms and his guitar on his back, he began walking down the street. We turned the corner and walked for at least five more blocks. Each step Isidro took sent a shooting pain up my leg, through my back and into my head. I closed my eyes and whimpered most of the way. Finally he stopped. I looked up and saw a building with pictures of other animals; dogs, cats, birds, even turtles and fish. It was an animal hospital!

As I lay in Isidro's arms, he struggled to reach for the door.

"Oh no, no, no," he said tiredly.

It was locked. They were closed. It was late in the day and almost everything was closed. Isidro quickly set me down. I thought, 'Ok this is it, he's done all that he can', but he reached into his pocket and pulled out his phone. He starred at the Animal Hospital sign and dialed the number on the sign while occasionally glancing down at me. I gave him my best sad look in hopes that he would not abandon me. He pushed his long hair back behind his ear and put the phone up to his ear. He looked down at me with a worried look. I could hear him say softly yet anxiously, "Come on, pick up, pick up".

Then I blacked out.

Chapter 4

The Longest Night

My body whole body felt numb except for the extreme pain in my leg and back. I tried to move but I could only lift my head. It was darker now and much colder. I laid there near dead on the driveway of the animal hospital. My body trembled from fear and the cold air. I was all alone. I tried so hard to get up, but I couldn't. I needed to get up. I remembered what happened to the injured dogs on the street. Now I was the injured one. I needed to find shelter. It must have been very late, because there were no people on the street. It was late and that's when the pack dogs roam.

Pack dogs are street dogs that choose to live together as a group to increase their chance of survival. They travel the streets looking for food. There is always one dominant male in the group. Usually he is the strongest and most aggressive. The rest of the group work together under the lead dog's commands. They can be dangerously vicious on the streets to other animals and, on occasion, to people. I have watched them from a distance. It is frightening what they can do when they work together.

My pain was unbearable. I wanted to cry, but knew I needed to keep as quiet as possible. I trembled with fear. I thought, 'If only I could crawl underneath that old truck down the street. The pack dogs would have a much harder time getting to me if I were under that truck.' I tried to get up, but I couldn't move.

I smelled them coming, long before I heard them. They were coming from downwind, a pack dog strategy. I tried to be still, but my body was shaking so hard from fear and pain. I shook so hard the gravel beneath me made noise. If only I could get to that old truck. With every bit of strength, I pulled myself with my two front paws. It seemed like maybe I was going to move until the gravel gave way and my paws slid deeper into the gravel. There was no hiding now. The noise gave up my location. I could hear the dogs now. It sounded like at least five, maybe as many as eight. They began to move around both sides of me in a zigzagging motion with their heads low to the ground. I could almost see them now. My eyes were wide open searching for their silhouettes moving in the dark. I had watched pack dogs before. They preferred hunting at night. They sometimes took hours to kill and devour their prey. Now I was in their sights, and there was little I could do to escape.

Startled by a deep dark growl I heard from behind me, I quickly turn my head. There he was! I had seen this dog before. He was a very large dog. A mix of pit bull and German shepherd with thick matted down hair. His head was scarred from street fights. He was the leader of the gang. He would come at me first, and then the others would follow. I thought about the best way to protect myself out in the open. I felt so vulnerable.

The other dogs soon came into view. They slipped in and out of the darkness and were on all sides of me now. Several of the dogs were growling and showing their teeth. My mind flipped back and forth from reality to fantasy. I thought about how to defend myself, and then I thought about my life back home under the porch. I thought about what it would take to kill the lead dog, and then I thought about chasing the birds that would drink from my water bowl. Suddenly I heard a deep growl and my mind shifted back to reality. Using all my strength I managed to roll over on my stomach so as to better protect my organs. I lifted my head as high as I could and growled back, but I was terrified.

I clearly saw them all now. There were six of them; the large lead male, two tall skinny black dogs, another grayish pit bull with a limp, and two smaller mixed dogs. The smell they gave off was horrible. It smelled like death.

The smaller ones came in first, but very strategically. They lunged in and out nipping at my tail and hind legs. I knew their strategy. They were meant to distract me from the bigger lead dog, and then when I wasn't looking the pit bull shepherd would come from the opposite direction. With his wide jaws he would make one quick deadly move. I saw it in his eyes now. He stared intently at my throat planning his attack. They all moved in a little closer sensing that I couldn't move. Each of them growling and nipping at me. I was so scared I no longer felt the pain from the accident. Then it happened.

The two tall skinny black dogs grabbed my one injured leg and began to pull me. I turned my head away from the lead dog to look down at my leg. Out of the corner of my eye I saw him leap with his mouth open wide. It was the most horrifying sight I could imagine. I closed my eyes. With all of his weight he pounced on me and clenched his jaws tightly around my throat.

When I opened my eyes I was in Isidro's arms again. He gently laid me down on a cold metal table. I looked up at him. He was smiling.

He said' "It's going to be ok girl."

There were no pack dogs, only Isidro and someone in a white coat. It was all a terrible dream, a nightmare really, and one that would recur often. Once on the table I felt a pinch in my backside, and in within seconds I fell back to sleep.

Chapter 5

The Healer

Dear Mom,

"It's gonna be OK," she said in a soft calming voice. "It's gonna be OK."

Over and over I heard those words as I awoke from a deep sleep. Her hand was slowly and gently stroking my head and neck. She was a young girl, short with long black hair and big brown eyes. She was dressed all in white. She stared down at me with a big affirming smile, as if what she was saying were actually true. Her smile was very comforting. I hadn't seen a person smile at me since I left home. I felt safe here.

As I stared back into her big brown eyes she turned away. "She's waking up Doctor Cruz."

A deep voice came from another room. "Good, but she's going be groggy for a while."

I turned my head to see who she was speaking to. My neck was sore and stiff. I struggled to see out of the corner of my eye. In walked a very tall, thin young man also dressed in white. He had a very serious look on his face, and gloves on his hands. He began adjusting a thin tube coming from what looked like a bag of water hanging from a pole. I followed the other end of the tube only to discover that it was attached to my paw!

"We'll keep her here for a while until she rehydrates," said the doctor, "She lost a lot of blood since the accident. Isidro said the accident happened around 7PM. I'm glad he was able to reach you Raquel, or she might have died".

"God was watching over her," Raquel replied.

I laid on that table all night with Raquel by my side. I drifted in and out of sleep. The table was hard and cold, but I was happy to be there. My body ached and I couldn't move my leg, but it was better than being on the streets.

The next morning Doctor Cruz returned. After greeting Raquel, he looked down at me and smiled. "So how is our new patient doing this morning?"

Raquel told him that I had slept off and on all night. Then he put on gloves and reached for my paw. He gently removed the tube from my leg.

"Let's see if we can get her to stand up."

Together they lifted me off the table onto the floor. I felt an intense pain in my back left leg and cried out! I struggled to stand on three legs. Again Raquel stroked my head saying, "Good girl"

I just stood there. I didn't know how to walk. It hurt too much. I stood there on three legs, the fourth just hanging. It was wrapped in a large brown bandage from my paw to the top of my leg.

"She'll figure it out," said the Doctor, "But it's going to take time. Hopefully her owners will be patient with her. Have you heard from them yet"?

"No, I haven't". Then she turned to me and said, "But we will, right girl?"

They were both so reassuring, but inside I felt scared. I had no owners looking for me. I was a street dog now. Maybe a three legged street dog. I had seen what happens to three legged dogs on the street. They don't last long. I tried not to think about it for now. I was focused on keeping my dangling leg from touching the ground and causing me pain. The pain had increased since Doctor Cruz removed the tube from my paw, and even more now that I was off the table.

Raquel brought a metal cage not much bigger than me and placed it next to where I was standing. They opened the door, and with a slight push from the Doctor, I hobbled inside and collapsed on my side. They closed the gate behind me. Together the two of them lifted my cage and carried me to another room with three other cages, two smaller ones and one my size. One of the smaller ones had a cat in it with a big white cone shaped thing around its head. It didn't seem to bother him, as he was fast asleep.

As Doctor Cruz and Raquel left the room I heard him say, "Give her some food and water. We'll give her owners a few days to come and find her." I knew that would never happen.

Chapter 6

Back on the Porch

Dear Mom,

I stayed in that cage at the doctor's office for days. I slept most of the time, and they would bring me food and water regularly. Raquel was especially nice to me. She talked to all the animals in their cages. Some came for only a few hours, some longer. I watched one dog die in his cage. Raquel wept that day.

She would always say to me, "Maybe your owners will come find you today."

I knew that wasn't true. I thought a lot about my old home and our owners while at the hospital. Sitting in a cage with a busted leg, there wasn't much else to do.

I remembered how we would lay on the front porch together at night waiting for our owner to get home. We would both be hungry. Sometimes it would be very late. That was never a good sign. The nights he was very late, we would listen closely for the sound of his truck pulling into the gravel driveway, watching for his headlights shining on the house next door as he made the turn. We wanted time to hide.

Our owner was a kind, hardworking man, but when he was out late, that usually meant he was drinking. When he drank he was often mean to you, Mom. As he pulled into the driveway we would scurry under the porch, always hoping he didn't see us. Out of sight out of mind, was our plan. Almost without fail he would stagger around the yard as if looking for something, only to step in a pile of poop.

"Tina!" He yelled.

He hopped on one foot towards the water hose to clean off the poop. You were always so obedient, Mom. You would crawl out from under the porch knowing he was going to kick you or spank you. In some ways you were his best friend in spite of all the abuse. It wasn't until I got older that he began to hit me.

I remember the first time. I was playing with a shoe our owner had left out on the porch. I was having a blast, but before you know it I had shredded the shoe almost unrecognizable. Afterwards I kept thinking, I hope our owner gets home early tonight. But he didn't. He came home very late and drunk. I was already hiding under the porch when I heard his old truck pull up. Within seconds he yelled my name at the top of his voice. I guess he knew you would never chew up his shoes, Mom. He knew right away it was me and continued yelling my name.

"Margarita, come here right now!"

I didn't want to come out, but I jumped and ran when he threw a stick under the porch. I ran to the far back corner of our property. He followed me with the shoe in one hand and a stick in the other. I curled up just before the first blow. He hit me several times while shaking the remains of the shoe in my face. The stick wasn't too painful. What hurt most was that I thought maybe someday, like you, Mom, I would be his best friend.

There were good days and bad days at home. As I lay here thinking about them, I hope you are well, Mom. I hope the good days outnumber the bad ones. In this small cage with a broken leg I feel like I am in limbo. I miss you, and part of me wants to be back on our porch. Yet, part of me is hopeful for something else.

Chapter 7

In the Cage

Dear Mom,

Well, it finally happened. I was fast asleep when Doctor Cruz and Raquel lifted my cage and carried it outside and set it on the back of a pickup truck. Neither of them said a word to me. The truck smelled like dog urine. Inside there were some large bags of dog food. They spoke to the driver, handed him some papers and shook his hand. They stared at me as we drove away.

The driver was a kind old man named Joseph. He took the main road up through the valley until I could no longer see the city. It got very bumpy and each bump caused pain to shoot up my leg. As we got further out of town I heard dogs barking, lots of them. As we got closer more dogs joined in. I had never heard so many dogs barking at once. Then I smelled them. It was all you could smell, not food, humans, or garbage, only dogs. The last hundred yards or so we went up a steep hill. Then Joseph stopped to open a gate, pulled the truck inside, and closed the gate behind us. I could barely see above the sides of the pickup truck.

Joseph opened the tail gate, pulled my cage towards him and set it on the ground. The dogs continued to bark.

Joseph yelled, "Be quiet!"

Some of the dogs stopped barking, but many continued. I still couldn't see any of them. The truck was between me and where the barking came from.

Joseph called out to a young man. He was cleaning dishes outside a small wooden shack. "Put her with the pups for now. "She's almost grown, but she's got a bum leg."

Joseph then got back in his truck and drove back towards the gate. As he pulled away all I could see were cages. They were all different sizes, some were half the size of our front porch, others were as big as our whole backyard, and everything in between. There were dozens of dogs, maybe even a hundred dogs.

The Shelter, as I later heard it called, sat up on a small hill outside of town. You could see the city in the distance. There was no grass, no trees, and no buildings except for the small wooden shack. There were only cages. From what I could see there were eight or ten different cages. Each cage was filled with dogs. Most of them were staring at me. It was frightening. My recurring dream was running through my head. Which cage would they put me in? How long would I be there? How long had the others been here?

The skinny young boy could barely lift my cage. He dropped me twice before finally setting me down next to one of the smaller cages. This particular cage had four young dogs. He opened their cage and pushed my crate up to the cage door. Then he opened the door on my crate and tilted it from behind, forcing me to roll out into the pen with the other dogs. I let out a yell as I rolled onto my broken leg. He quickly closed the gate behind me.

Good boy." He said.

'Hellooo….I'm a girl,' I thought to myself.

To my amazement I stood right up for the first time in days. It must have been instinct. I didn't want to appear weak to the other dogs. I couldn't put my full weight on that leg, but I could get around. The other dogs were very curious and began snooping and sniffing around me. I gave them a quick growl and they backed away. I was scared in my new surroundings, but I took some comfort in the fact that I was bigger than the four dogs in my cage. At least I had that going for me. More than once my height has kept me out of trouble, despite feeling scared on the inside. I found a cozy place in the corner and claimed it for myself. From there I spent the rest of the day watching the pups play, and listening to an occasional fight going on in the other pens.

I quickly learned the routine. They fed us twice a day and they cleaned the pens every other day. The food varied a lot. We rarely got the same meal twice. Lots of old tortillas mixed with beans, corn and whatever other vegetables arrived that day. They mixed it up in a wheel barrel, pushed it around to the different pens and filled all the dishes. It always got real loud at feeding time. Some days we got very little. I heard Joseph talk about the local mining company that funded the shelter. He said that sometimes if the mine wasn't making any money, they wouldn't send any food for the dogs. All of the dogs at the shelter were very skinny, and when the food was low they got even skinnier. Some died. Most were already sick, and when there was little food they couldn't survive.

I remember the first time I saw a dog at the shelter die. It was one of those weeks were there was almost no food available. They fed us once a day and it was mainly old tortillas mixed with water. This poor dog had been sick for days. She came into the shelter sick and never got better. When there's no money, there's no medicine either. She was sad looking when she arrived. She was young, but looked old. Her dark brown hair was dirty and matted down. She walked very slowly with a limp, but most of the time she just laid next to the fence. Her eyes were covered with so many bugs that she could barely open them. Her stomach was bloated. They put her in the pen next to mine. She hardly moved except to get up at meal time. Shortly after eating she would begin choking and vomit up her food. One morning she never woke up.

I wondered what they would do with her after she died. I watched and waited. It wasn't until feeding time in the afternoon that they discovered her dead body. We were being fed only once a day at that time. Joseph went into the pen with a wheel barrel and gently placed her inside. He pushed the wheel barrel to the side of the shack where he had built a fire. Hanging above the fire was a huge pot. You could see the steam rising from the pot. I sat in amazement as Joseph used a large machete to cut the flesh from that poor dog and add it to the pot, piece by piece. It was horrifying! Joseph set his small chair next to the fire and sat down. On occasion he would add wood to the fire, or stir the pot with his big walking stick. The air slowly filled with the smell of food and some of the dogs began to bark.

Joseph yelled, "Be quiet"!

Joseph stayed by that pot all night long, occasionally stirring and adding some other things. Fourteen hours after they found that poor dog dead in the pen, they served it to all the dogs. We were all starving and were so happy to have real food. I think more dogs would have died that week if Joseph had not provided that meat. What looked like a cruel act saved the lives of other dogs. I wondered how many other dogs had died at the shelter and been used for food.

Chapter 8

Freedom

Dear Mom,

My leg is almost all healed! Doctor Cruz came to visit me a few weeks ago and took off the last of the bandages. He takes care of all the sick dogs here. I have a pretty good limp, but it seems to be slowly improving. He told Joseph that if the owners had picked me up and cared for me right after the accident, I would have had a better chance of healing without a limp. I don't blame our owners though, Mom. It was my choice to leave home.

Eventually I was moved to another pen with some of the bigger and less aggressive dogs. That's how they divided us up here. There were some dogs that were very mean and had to be isolated. There was the puppy pen where I started out. There were some dogs that were always anxious and fearful. Some were just not friendly and couldn't get along. There was a pen for each group. I was in the playful pen. Everyone in my pen was pretty easy going. One big advantage of my new pen is what happens when someone comes to adopt a dog. It's the best pen to be in on adoption day, because Joseph always brought them to our pen first. Unless of course they wanted a guard dog, the kind that lived in a cage, or tied to a chain outside of the house. Those folks he took straight to the mean dog's pen.

Weeks went by and occasionally one of the dogs in my pen would leave with a new owner. One time they brought the poor pooch back. I heard he couldn't adjust to life outside and he destroyed his new owner's fence trying to get back to the shelter. How sad. He traded his freedom for the cage.

Every time someone came to my pen they would say the same thing. "Look how pretty she is. Her eyes are gorgeous... Oh no, she has a limp". Then they would turn away. After several months I had given up hope of ever being adopted. My limp got a little better, but it never completely healed. I accepted that I would always have a limp and that no one would adopt a dog with a limp when they could pick one without.

Then, one hot summer day in the middle of the afternoon, an older couple came to my pen looking for a dog. They were older and spoke funny. In fact I couldn't understand a word they were saying. Turns out they weren't Mexican, they were from the USA. But even speaking another language, I knew that familiar look once they spotted my limp. Eventually Joseph took them to another pen where they chose an older dog. She was bigger and less friendly, more of the guard dog type. I guess that's what they wanted, a guard dog. To my surprise two days later they returned with that black shepherd in their car. Joseph took the shepherd and put him back in its' pen. When Joseph's helper ask the American man what happened, he replied, "She would hardly eat and she laid in the same spot near the door for two days". She was another dog that couldn't adjust to life outside the cages.

Before leaving the couple walked around my pen looking at all the dogs. There were six of us in my pen. I was the tallest, but the others could get up on the fence on their hind legs better than me. I would climb up on my hind legs to get noticed like the other dogs, but couldn't stay as long and dropped back down to all fours.

The woman kept pointing at me and smiling. She would then look at the man and say "Pleeeez John."

He would point at my leg and say something back to her while shaking his head no. Then John closed his eyes and stood still for a moment. When he opened his eyes he took the woman's hand and turned to walk away. As they walked towards their car John called for Joseph. They spoke at the car a few minutes and then returned to my pen. Joseph had a leash in his hand when he opened the gate. Someone was getting out.

The other dogs ran to the gate. I followed, but had little hope of being chosen. It was always one of the others that got chosen. They were all barking and jumping onto Joseph's leg. He pushed them aside.

"Be quiet!" he yelled.

He was heading straight for me! He looked me right in the eyes, tapped his leg with his big hand and said, "Come girl." For a brief moment I couldn't move. I thought I was dreaming. Then I sprung up so fast that I fell down in a cloud of desert dust.

Joseph turned to the American couple and said, "She has one leg that is still healing, so she's a little clumsy."

I thought, 'Thanks Joseph, you just ruined any chance of my being adopted.' I quickly got to my feet and ran to Joseph. Outside the cage I heard the couple laughing at my graceful exit. As Joseph attached the leash and walked me out of the cage, I made my best effort not to limp.

John approached me slowly and knelt down in front of me to get a better look at me. I thought I should try and look tough, since these folks were looking for a guard dog. But I was so excited that I pushed my nose into John's face and began licking his face and neck. John kept looking back at the woman. He spoke something to her, and she kept shaking her head yes. I couldn't understand what they were saying.

Then I heard John say, "Ok Pat."

He rose to his feet, shook Joseph's hand and took a hold of the leash. As he walked me towards their car I wondered, is this really happening? John opened the back hatch of the car and signaled for me to jump in. I knew it was too high for me. Even if I could make it, I knew it would be very painful. With all my might I leaped for the car. I fell short and hung there with only my head, upper chest and two front paws in the car, my butt and two hind legs dangled in the air. John quickly pushed up on my rear and I scrambled the rest of the way in, trying to act like nothing happened.

John and Pat looked at each other. Then I heard John say sarcastically in rough Spanish, "My guard dog," and they both laughed.

John closed the hatch. He and Pat climbed into the front seats and off we went. As we approached the gate I looked out the back window at the other dogs. Slowly their barks diminished. I watched out the window until I no longer saw the shelter.

Chapter 9

New Owners

Dear Mom,

I will never forget my first day at my new owner's house. It was exciting and scary at the same time. I wondered, would I only last a day or two like some of the other dogs at the shelter? Would my new owners treat me better than our owner treated you, Mom? Would I want to run away again? How would things be different in my new home? Would I be happy here?

Driving down the hill towards the city, I had all of these thoughts running through my head. It felt great to be out of the sun. In fact, it felt strangely cool. It was a very hot summer day, but inside their car it was cool, almost cold. This was my first time inside a car. I learned later that they can control the temperature in cars. My new life was off to a good start already, less heat. John drove the car towards the city center. It had been a while since I was in the city. We passed some familiar places. I saw the park with the slide where I spent my first night on the streets. I recognized the animal hospital when we passed by. As we got near to their house, you'll never believe who I saw. It was Isidro on his motorcycle! He passed right next to our car. He was going so fast that I'm sure he never saw me. I thought to myself, if he doesn't slow down he's going to get hit by a car and end up in the hospital, just like I did.

After the short drive we arrived at their home. John opened the hatch and removed my leash. I stumbled gracefully as I descended from their SUV. This was the first time out of a cage and off of a leash in months. My new owner, Pat, was talking to me, but I was in explore mode. With my nose barely an inch off the ground I spent the next 15 minutes zigzagging my way over every inch of the property. It was all concrete except for a small patch of dirt with a tiny tree planted in the middle of it. I could smell the dog that was there before me. Of course that was my main reason for explore mode. I needed to know if there were any other animals here. The place was clean. No animals in sight, or smell. I began to relax a bit. Pat brought me out a bowl of water, and later on some food. At night they gave me a blanket to sleep on. They put it on the patio, but I dragged it up onto the front porch and fell fast asleep.

Over the next few months I learned to trust my new owners. They never knew my name was Margarita, so they gave me a new one. After some discussion they settled on

Daisy. It took me a while to figure out that my name had been changed. I liked my new name, and my new owners.

They continued to speak English around the house, but spoke Spanish when we went out into the community. They took a lot of time to teach me things, and I quickly began to learn their commands in English. In contrast, learning where to pee and poop seemed to take me forever. My new owners were pretty adamant about me peeing and pooping only in the small area of dirt inside the patio walls. This seemed pretty ridiculous to me. I'll decide where I want to pee and poop. But they wouldn't have that. They kept the patio very neat and clean. Eventually after I did a little late night tree removal, I went along with the plan. Not being able to understand the language I became a really good listener. I slowly figured it out. John and Pat used to tell people that I was the only bilingual dog in town. One day I learned what 'Daisy' meant; it's a flower, Mom. Do you know what they call that flower in Spanish? Margarita! How could they have known that?! Life was different here. Better.

John and Pat were very patient with me. I chewed up the first few blankets they gave me to sleep on. I completely destroyed a nice bed they bought for me, and dug up Pat's flowers so many times, they eventually made it into a rock garden. I got my share of spankings, but I always sensed that it wasn't that they wanted to harm me, but that they wanted me to learn. There was this one time when John spent hours building this little wooden house. It was not much bigger than me. After he finished, he put my blanket inside the little wooden house. Why did he do that? He called me over and told me to get in the box he built. Why would I want to go in there? I'll stay right here thank you. He lifted my front end and gently pushed me from behind in an effort to get me in the small wooden box. I was almost completely inside when I spun my head back out the door and bit the palm of John's hand. I bit him just hard enough to let him know who was in charge. Well, I found out pretty quick who was really in charge, and it wasn't me. I got my worst spanking that day.

Later that day John wrote, "Daisy" above the opening in the box. That night when I went to go to sleep, I couldn't find my blanket. The nights were getting colder and the blanket helped to keep me warm on the cold concrete. Then I remembered that John put my blanket in the box. I crawled into the box to get my blanket and discovered how much warmer it was inside the box. Once I curled up inside, it got even warmer from my body heat. I felt bad about biting John. He had made this little house for me to keep warm at night. I learned to trust that my owners would do what was best for me. Over and over again they proved to be very caring.

Chapter 10

Old Habits Die Hard

Dear Mom,

My new home is a nice 4 room house. There's a good size patio on two sides of the house. John and I play with the ball out there a lot. The house and patio are surrounded by an eight-foot rock wall. Sometimes at night cats would walk on top of the walls to get from one house to the other. This always got me fired up. I would bark and growl and jump at the wall, but it never seemed to bother them. Those cats are pretty smart. The rock wall made it pretty easy to guard the house. There was only one door to get inside the wall. Outside that door was the city. Inside the door was my territory.

I learned to be a pretty good guard dog. My owners were worried I wouldn't be. At first I used to hear them say, "how come she never barks" and "when is she going to bark". They didn't know that dogs have to care about someone before they will protect them.

"She's a great guard dog." I've heard them tell people, "We don't know how she does it, but she knows if the person outside the wall is supposed to be there or not."

Sometimes John would leave the door open while bringing in groceries from the car. There were a few times I slipped out. The smells and sights of the street would cause me to forget about everything else, and in a minute or two I was halfway down the street, or all the way up the alley that ran alongside the house. I could hear John yelling my name.

"Daisy come!" He called over and over.

It was like something took over my body and all I wanted was to be on the street sniffing where other dogs peed and picking though garbage. John's voice was like a whisper compared to the fury of thoughts in my head. With my nose close to the ground I wandered further away from home. Eventually John caught up to me and grabbed me by my collar. He held that collar tight all the way home. When we got home he tied me to a post on the patio. He called it a "time out." It took me a while, but I learned to only go outside on the leash with John or Pat.

I loved when Pat went jogging and took me with her. She ran for miles! It was great. Some days were so hot though that I barely made it back home. First thing she did when we got back was give me a giant bowl of fresh water. I gulped it down while she drank her drink.

I have learned a lot the past few months. I had to work at it. John and Pat spent a lot of time teaching me things. I have grown so much, and gotten fatter too. The food has been pretty awesome, especially the leftovers! Oh my gosh, I would inhale that stuff. So I put on a few pounds. Except for this one sore on my tail that won't go away, I'm in great shape.

P.S. Remember the recurring nightmare I told you about, the one where the pack of dogs attacked me? Well the dreams have stopped. It's been over six months. Yea!

Chapter 11

A 50/50 Chance

Dear Mom,

Everything was going really well. I was learning so much and enjoying my new home. I loved spending time with my new owners and their friends. I was growing stronger, or so I thought. I felt like I was given a new life, like I was on top of the mountain. Do you remember that sore I told you about in my last letter, the one on my tail? It never went away. Pat tried putting medicine on it, but it didn't help. Soon I had them all over my body. They began as bumps, some as small as a pea, others the size of a small ball, then they opened up into sores that bled. They hurt and made me feel tired.

They took me to see Dr. Cruz. It was good to see him and Raquel again. John held me down while Dr. Cruz put a needle in my front left leg. He said he was going to test my blood. I didn't know what that meant.

Dr. Cruz always had a pretty serious face, but this time was different. He looked at John and Pat and said, "She has cancer."

I understood what he said before they did. They were still learning Spanish and they asked Dr. Cruz to repeat what he said two more times. Then John said, "Dogs can get cancer?"

I thought the same thing. I had heard of humans being sick and even dying from cancer. Now I had it. Pat began to cry. I laid there in shock, while John and Pat talked with Dr. Cruz about what to do.

A few months ago I learned that John and Pat had another dog before me. Not the one they returned after two days, but another one they had for about a year. Her name was Bella. Not long before they got me she got hit by a car and died. It broke Pat's heart. She was sad for weeks. As I laid there in the animal hospital John and Pat argued about what to do. Dr. Cruz said he had some medicine, but that it was about a 50/50 chance that I would live even with the medicine. They continued to argue, but not because of the price. Dr. Cruz said he had a special medicine he called chemotherapy, and that is was due to expire. He had to use it soon, or throw it away. The bigger issue for John was burying another dog. John did not want Pat get attached to another dog and then watch it die. They talked about taking me back to the shelter and getting another dog.

Pat looked at John with tears rolling down her cheeks. "Daisy is our responsibility now. We can't abandon her when she needs us most."

John looked down for a moment with his eyes closed. I had seen him do this before. Finally, he looked up at Dr. Cruz. "What should we do next, Doc?"

Dr. Cruz explained the process of my treatment. My owners would have to bring me every week for six weeks for an hour of chemotherapy treatment, beginning next Tuesday.

Pat said, "No problem, I will have her here every week."

I had mixed feelings. I was glad they decided not to take me back to the shelter, but I still only had a 50/50 chance. I could not understand why this happened when things in my life were finally going so good.

Two days before my first treatment Pat had to leave Mexico unexpectedly, and would be gone for many weeks. Day by day I grew more tired and the sores became more painful. After my visit with Dr. Cruz, John began giving me several pills every day. I lost my appetite. By the first day of treatment I was very weak. John lifted me into the back of the car and off we went.

They were waiting for us, so John placed me right up onto the doctors table. I was so scared I peed all over the table. John brought lots of my favorite treats to distract me while the doctor hooked a tube up to my leg. For the next 45 minutes John held me tight, petting me and feeding me the treats while Dr. Cruz slowly administered the chemotherapy. For the next six weeks John and I visited Dr. Cruz. I got so tired after the treatments. Sometimes I threw up. Then it happened. The sores were going away! The bumps were getting smaller! It took a while but even the worst one that started it all, the one on my tail completely healed. John and I grew close in the process, but I couldn't wait to see Pat. She would be so happy. I am so thankful for her compassion. I will never forget her words, "Daisy is our responsibility."

Chapter 12

Letting Go

Dear Mom,

I can't believe it's been over a year since I left home. Some days it feels like it's been longer, other times it feels like just yesterday. My birthday came and went. My owners didn't know it was my birthday so it was just like any other day for them. I did go on a really cool hike with John deep into the desert that day. We do that a lot now that I am feeling better. Pat returned just after the New Year and she brought someone with her.

When Pat stepped out of the car she had tears in her eyes. She hugged me so tight. A young woman came around from the other side of the car. She had a big smile and pretty blue eyes.

She looked at me and said "Hi, Daisy." I tilted my head and wagged my tail. "Come, Daisy." She was trying to make friends, but for a brief moment I just stood there.

Then I heard Pat say, "Go say hi to Joanna, Daisy."

I skipped across the patio towards her. Joanna stooped down and gave me a hug. I later learned that Joanna was one of John and Pats two daughters that live in the United States. Joanna came and stayed with us for almost six months.

It was great to have Joanna at the house. She and I would play for hours, she taught me tricks, and she even snuck me into the house to sleep on the bed with her a few times. As spring came to an end their other daughter Stephanie came to visit for almost 2 months. The house was so busy, with lots of activities. When John wasn't working, we would all go on long hikes together. Sometimes we all piled into the car and went to the beach. I was a little scared of the water, but I loved running on the sand. I would run for hours at the beach or on our hikes. My leg usually hurt the next day, but that didn't stop me.

Those were great days, but they came to an end when their daughters returned to the USA. John and Pat got very sad when they left, especially Pat. I think men are wired different than women. It's hard to put into words, but it's like sometimes they're afraid to show their feelings. I tried my best to cheer them up, and I think I helped. It was hard to see their girls leave. It was hard to let go.

I wasn't going to share this in my letter but I need to tell you something. A few weeks ago John took me for a ride. I often go for rides with him. He always says, "Go for a ride Daisy?" Then I run to the car and hop in the second he opens the door.

We delivered some food to a family on the other side of town. They were a really nice family. They had a small, one room house with a dirt floor. There was a blanket hung from the ceiling across the middle of the room to separate where they slept. Afterwards John took me for a walk in the nice people's neighborhood. In this part of town there was very little traffic and John let me walk without the leash. As we walked the streets I got a little ahead of John. I liked being the leader. Walking past a row of hedges I smelled a familiar smell. Then it hit me…that smell. I turned to my right and there you were! I was in front of our house! I froze. I could see you sleeping under the porch. I wanted to scream as loud as I could but I didn't. From the corner of my eye I saw our old owner working on his truck. I stood there in silence. John had caught up to me and proceeded to pass me.

He said "Come on girl," as he continued on ahead of me.

I stood and stared at you, Mom. A flood of emotions ran over me. It was such a joy to see you, but at the same time I was sad. I saw your owner working on the truck and remembered how he treated you. For a moment I was going to bark so you would see me and know that I was

OK. Then I thought if the owner saw me, he might try to keep me there. I didn't know what to do.

As I stood outside the fence I heard John's voice from off in the distance. "Come on Daisy, let's go home and see mommy." I knew I had to go. I turned and walked up the sidewalk a few feet and stopped again. I took a final look back at you, and let go.

As I caught up to John he said, "Good girl Daisy, good girl." It didn't feel so good at the time, but I knew it was what I had to do.

Chapter 13

Walking On Water

Dear Mom,

I'm sorry I haven't written in a while. I hope you're not mad at me. I guess it's part of letting go. But also there's been so much going on. John and Pat sure get a lot more visitors than we ever did.

It seems like there is always someone coming over the house, or to John's office. They have a small office that's not attached to the house. Sometimes they let me hang out in there. Sometimes a group of moms will come over and work on stuff with Pat. Sometimes a group of guys will come over and talk for hours with John. I like when the moms come, because they always bring their children. Some of the kids are even smaller than me. I love playing with the kids. They have so much more energy than John or Pat. They can play for hours and not get tired. They do cry a lot though, over the littlest things. Sometimes larger groups come for celebrations, or what they call movie night. Best thing about movie night is all the snacks the kids spill on the patio are mine. Then there are a few occasions where groups of people come and stay for a week or more. John and Pat feed them and give them a place to sleep. These are some of the nicest folks. John and Pat love it because they can speak English with the people. Some of them come from as far as Canada.

Once the weather got hot again, John and Pat started taking me on daytrips with them. John loves to drive his car out into the wilderness. Often we end up near a river, or a deserted beach. Pat usually brings food along and a couple of chairs. I love being able to wander off with no cars, houses, or people around. It's always very calming.

One day we drove out to this shallow river where John and I had hiked several times before. This time we went to an area where the water was deeper. I loved running through the water, but once it was over my knees I would turn around. This water was so deep that it was over Johns head. I began to worry about him and Pat out there so I began bark. John was calling for me to come to him. I would head out a few feet but no further. Finally John came up to the shore. I was less nervous with him out of the water.

As I watched Pat walking towards the river bank, I felt John pick me up. Was he putting me back in the car? Did I bark too much? Instead he walked straight to the river bank and threw me into the water as far as he could. My eyes were wide open as I flew through the air, and in an instant I went from flying to swimming, two things I had never done before. Just like John, my head never went under the water, even though my feet couldn't touch the ground. Without even thinking my legs instinctively began to paddle under the water.

I could hear John laughing as Pat began to shout, "Swim to me Daisy, swim to me". I paddled over to Pat and she grabbed me and hugged me. John got back into the water and I swam over to him. I spent the next half hour swimming back and forth between the two of them. This was awesome! It's like I was weightless. Even my leg felt better under water.

Later that afternoon John taught me fetch in the water. We played on the patio all the time, but this was different. He would throw a stick way out into the water. I would jump in, swim out to the stick, put it between my teeth and swim all the way back to the river bank and give John the stick. Boy, did I sleep great that night. In fact it was the first time I ever fell asleep in the back of the car. What a day!

I remember lying in bed that night thinking about how scared I used to be of the deep water. If John hadn't thrown me in the river, I never would have known the excitement and thrill of moving through the water. That's what swimming is, Mom. It was like walking with no feet on the ground. I have no idea what held me up. It was like I walked on water.

Chapter 14

The Places I Got Hurt

Dear Mom,

I think of you often and hope you are well. I know you have a hard time keeping warm now that winter is here again. The desert winds at night are the worst part. Days like these always remind me of the day I got hit by the car. I will never forget that day. A few weeks ago John and I walked down the street where I got hit by the car. Of course John didn't know where I got hit, but as soon as I turned the corner I froze. John tugged on my leash and I proceeded, but it felt very eerie walking down that street. A lot of memories came rushing back. About half way down the block with my head down I began to pick up the pace, pulling John behind me. I was thankful to be alive, but I didn't need to hang around that street very long. We continued on and I never looked back.

I'm almost three years old now, Mom. In dog years I'm an adult now. I don't tear things up the way I used to. I learned to stop chewing everything in sight. I even stopped digging up Pat's plants, what few she had left. Actually it had nothing to do with the plants, although that's what

John and Pat probably thought. You see at night, they would leave the patio lights on as a deterrent for potential intruders. But the lights attracted insects, and the insects attracted lizards, and I loved catching lizards. Sometimes they ran for cover in Pat's plants. I knew better than to dig in the plants, but I would get so caught up in the frenzy that I lost all reason. All that mattered was catching that lizard. So I would dig until I got him. I liked to catch them alive and play with them. I would toss them up in the air, push them around with my paw, give them a little head start then catch them again. They are great fun until they die.

John used to say, "Look Pat, Daisy has a 'mascota'. Are you playing with your mascota Daisy?" Which of course means 'pet' in English. John liked practicing his Spanish around me. He used to tell people that I was a bilingual dog and laugh. Little did he know.

One day my habit of playing with lizards and insects got me into some real trouble. John and Pat loaded up some things in the car and headed off without me. Shortly after they left I got bored and began looking for something to do. I strolled over to my water bowl. Often the pigeons, or small birds would sneak a drink when I wasn't looking.

Once I caught a bird in mid-air. By the time he saw me coming it was too late. He took off but I jumped up and caught him in my mouth. It chirped so loud that Pat came out side to see what the noise was. She called, "John, Daisy has a bird, and it's still alive!" She turned to me and said, "Daisy no, no Daisy." I never understood why humans always say things twice to dogs. Long story short, John took the bird from me before I ever got to play with it. That would have been fun.

Anyway, as I got closer to my bowl I noticed two very small birds or two very large insects. They told me later they were hornets. They looked like potential mascotas to me. I stood still. I began to crouch down. I was pretty sure I could get to them in one big leap. To my surprise they never moved when I jumped and snatched them from the bowl with my mouth. I quickly lifted my head from the bowl and moved toward the porch when I felt the first sting. My mouth sprung open and as I shook my head I felt a second sting. I shook them both out and off they flew. My tongue began to burn with pain. I ran for my water bowl, but the water didn't help. I had never felt pain like this before. It hurt so bad I began rubbing my tongue in the small patch of dirt hoping it would help. It got slightly better. The pain reduced from a constant stabbing feeling to a very painful throbbing. I laid on the patio panting hard. I hoped the worst of it was over, but it wasn't.

Before long, my tongue began to swell. Eventually it got so big that it hung way out of my mouth. I began to choke. I got up and began to swinging my head from side to side hoping to get some air in my throat. If I swung my head real hard my tongue would push just far enough to one side to let a tiny bit of air in. Then I would swing my head again hoping to catch another bit of air. I struggled to breathe as my tongue was four or five times its normal size now. I choked as I moved around the patio swinging my swollen tongue from side to side catching tiny bits of air. I began to give up hope when I heard Pat's voice. She was outside the door to the patio. In my state of confusion I never even heard their car.

She said, "I'm just going to make sure I turned the coffee pot off." She opened the door and saw me walking in circles swinging my head from side to side.

She quickly yelled' "John come quick, there's something wrong with Daisy!"

John came running in and they stood staring in shock. There I was walking in circles choking and scratching at my tongue. John picked me up and carried me to the car. They sped all the way to the vet and laid me on the familiar table.

They asked Dr. Cruz, "What happened, what's wrong with her"?

"It looks like an insect bite on her tongue and she's having an allergic reaction."

The doctor quickly filled a syringe and gave me an injection in my hind leg that made my whole body go numb. I continued to gasp for air, but I couldn't move and couldn't feel a thing. I was wide awake, but it's like I was out of my body. I hovered above the room looking down at myself. I could see Pat crying. I watched the doctor fill another syringe and inject it directly into my tongue. Was I dying? I felt no pain and could see everything clearly. I watched Dr. Cruz fill a third syringe and again injected it into my tongue.

"It's going down," said John, "The swelling is going down."

I felt my lungs begin to fill with air again. My breathing began to slow down to a normal rate. I blinked my eyes and looked up at Pat. She was still crying. I was back on the table again. I couldn't move, but I knew I was alive. I slowly regained my perspective and the feeling in my body, including the incredible pain in my mouth. My tongue returned to normal size, but it sure did hurt.

After a few more minutes the three of us walked slowly back to the car. I barely moved on the ride home. Once on the patio I went right for my water bowl; I was so thirsty. After a drink I went and laid down in my doghouse and slept for hours. When I awoke it was night time. I sat on the patio looking up at the sky and it hit me: I almost died today. My walk with John a few weeks ago reminded me that I almost died in the car accident. Then there was the cancer. I must be the luckiest dog on the planet. I've heard it said that cats have nine lives. Well, I'm on number four. Like I said Mom, I'm almost three years old now, an adult. This experience made me realize there is more to life than chasing lizards and chewing up blankets. I had been given a huge gift. Staring up at the stars that night, I had a new perspective. I can't fully describe it yet, but I think I'm ready for whatever comes next.

Chapter 15

A Boat Ride

Dear Mom,

I am hoping you receive this letter, because my owners have moved. Not just to another part of town, but to a whole other part of Mexico! I was worried that maybe they wouldn't take me with them, but they did. My new town is called Hermosillo. It's not a town like Santa Rosalia. It's a huge city filled with people and cars and buildings. I've never seen anything like it. Remember in my last letter I told you that I was ready for whatever comes next? Well I wasn't ready for this.

John and Pat began talking about moving to another place for their work a few months prior to our move. They talked about a few cities, but then they decided on Hermosillo. They have a friend named Gustavo that works there. For weeks Pat was packing boxes and cleaning the house. They had a small trailer in their enclosed patio that I never saw them use except for storing stuff. "Ministry supplies", John called them. John pushed the trailer out onto the street and began to fill it with all the belongings. He even put stuff on top of that little white trailer. Then he filled the car and put stuff on top of the car. My place in the back was full of stuff. Where was I going to sit? Maybe they weren't going to take me? Maybe I was going back to the shelter? It was a nerve racking couple of days for me.

One morning they both woke up very early and put the last of their things in the car. Pat put my leash on me and walked out to the street. They locked the door behind them. Several neighbors came out to say goodbye. Maci who ran the hardware store next door spoke while the others bowed their heads. I was so anxious that I needed to pee. I thought I better wait until I find out what's going on. Pat gave the leash to John and she got in the passenger side of the car where she always sits. She always preferred John driving. That's a whole other story that I'll tell you another time, Mom. The only space left in the car was the two front seats where John and Pat always sat. Pat left the door open. John shook hands with Maci and some others and walked over to close Pat's door.

Pat said, "Come on Daisy, you're coming too." I jumped into her lap. "Oh my gosh!" said Pat, "not on my lap Daisy."

She eased me down into a small place she saved for me next to her feet. I was pretty squished down there on the floor by Pat's feet along with a couple small bags and a gallon jug of water. John climbed into the driver's seat and we drove off waving to our neighbors. A sense of relief came over me. I was sure I wasn't going back to the shelter now. I thought, "They must be taking me to Hermosillo with them, but where on earth is Hermosillo? How long will I be in the car? I should have peed before I got in the car."

Turns out we weren't in the car very long at all. In fact we only drove down to the harbor. There was a ferry boat docked in the harbor. John got out of the car and handed the boat captain some papers and some pesos. He got back in and drove the car and trailer right inside the boat. I had seen plenty of fishing boats on our beach trips, but this boat was huge. Not only did our car and trailer fit, it held at least twenty more cars and trucks. We got out of the car together and John took a hold of my leash. The three of us walked through a small door and went down a narrow hall. There were lots of people boarding the boat and the hall was quite crowded. I was pretty nervous. I wasn't too sure about this whole boat thing. I considered myself a fine swimmer, but inside this hallway I wouldn't even be able to get to the water.

At the end of the hall was another door on the right. We turned to enter and immediately in front of me was a dark, very steep staircase. I had never seen steps like that before, and I had never gone down any. The hotel downtown had some out front, but nothing like this dark tunnel going down to who knows where. I stopped dead in my tracks. People hurried by me going up and down.

John headed down the steep staircase and said, "Come on girl, it's OK." I was not going down there. I panicked. John pulled the leash a bit hoping I would follow. At the same time I jerked my head in the opposite direction. In that moment my collar came loose. I was free! I didn't have to go down those awful steps. I ran back down the hallway, out the door and was headed for the boat ramp. Then I stopped. Where would I go? Why would I leave John and Pat? In that moment I remembered my night under the stars, the night I almost died from the hornet stings. Was this the thing I didn't understand that night?

As I stood on the edge of the boat thinking, a young man came up from behind me and slipped my collar around my neck. He had picked it up and ran after me. Holding me by the collar he walked me back down the long hall where John stood waiting. He looked frustrated, but I sensed he understood my fear. He knew I had never gone down stairs like this before. He quickly lifted me up from behind around my abdomen and headed down the stairs holding me three feet off the ground with my four legs facing forward.

I was all in now, but that didn't make it any less scary. People continued to go up and down around us. In my moment of fear, my bladder let loose. Being three feet off the ground and going down the steep staircase caused my pee to shoot at least six or eight feet out in front of me. I peed the entire way down the stairs. John would maneuver me to the left or right trying to direct my pee from hitting any of the people coming and going. Pat screamed as she watched me pee a perfectly arched stream all the way down the steps.

John let out a deep growling groan, the kind he often used when frustrated, then repeatedly said to passersby, "I'm so sorry."

At the bottom of the stairs John set me down and we walked to a very small room they called a cabin. Inside there was a three foot by three foot floor space and a set of bunk beds. Pat proceeded to put newspaper down for me in case I had to pee. "No need for that," I thought, "I'm good now."

It was quite a while before the boat left shore. Pat brought me food and my blanket. It was an old boat and turns out they had some mechanical issues, but eventually we got under way. You could tell because the whole room moved up and down and back and forth. I was scared but got used to it. It was a long ride. John and Pat tried to sleep, but they were kind of anxious too.

We arrived the next morning. I got back into my little spot in the car near Pat's feet and drove for several hours. Wherever we were, it was hot, hotter than Santa Rosalia and you know how hot that is, Mom. Sometimes I would climb up on Pat's lap to look around. We drove through a big desert. They call it the Sonora desert. Finally, we came to Hermosillo. There were so many cars. I sensed John was nervous. He kept looking back at his trailer and always checking his mirrors. There were cars all around him the whole time in the city.

We pulled into the driveway of a pretty white house on the corner of a quieter neighborhood.

Smiling, John turned to Pat and said, "We made it." Together we explored inside the house and the patio. It was very, very nice. Over the next few weeks we all adjusted to our new home. I sensed John and Pat were less relaxed here than in Santa Rosalia. They were very concerned about security. I had to step up my guard dog game. I wanted to help them be more at ease, to not worry about someone trying to break in. I was learning something very important, something that Pat modeled for me when I had cancer, and she told John that I was their responsibility now. I began to understand that John and Pat were my responsibility.

Chapter 16

Man's Best Friend

Dear Mom,

It has been an adjustment moving to Hermosillo. The hardest part was getting used to the heat. This is a big city. My owners are much busier here. Sometimes they go away for days, even weeks at a time. In Santa Rosalia when they went away, the next door neighbor brought me food and water every day. In my new city, they take me to pet hotels when they go out of town. Some of them were better than others.

The worst pet hotel I stayed at was called Mascota Spa. Let me tell you, it was no spa. I spent most of my time in a three by four cage. Three times a day they would let us out for twenty minutes to pee and poop. Some dogs couldn't hold their pee that long and they peed in their cage. The whole place smelled like pee. Four days later they picked me up. A day after I got home, I began coughing. My new vet said I caught kennel cough. I had to take a pill twice a day for ten days. It finally went away. They never took me to that hotel again.

The best pet hotel I stayed at was called The Woof Club. This place was awesome! It didn't start out so awesome. John gave my leash to a nice lady and Pat hugged me goodbye. The nice lady took me behind the counter and handed me to her husband Victor. He then brought me into the next room, a small garage. I thought, 'Oh no, this can't be good. So much for the Woof Club being a spa, it looks more like Club Carport.'

There was a van in the garage. Victor opened the side door and put me in a small cage that was in the van. There was another dog in the cage next to me, a small, well-groomed Pug. Looking at Pugs always cracked me up. Their face looks like they got hit in the face with a shovel. He was a happy little shovel-faced fella. Together old shovel face and I drove off with Victor.

I wondered where we were we going. It was almost a thirty minute drive. When the door opened all I saw was open space. Shovel face and I hopped out of the van to explore Club Carport. Boy, was I wrong. Like I said, this place was awesome. There were five other dogs already at The Woof Club. At night we each had our own room to sleep in, and they were big rooms. During the day we roamed free and played with other dogs. They even had a small pond to play in the water. Shovel face and I quickly made friends. Everyone at the Woof Club got along really well. Some days Victor brought new dogs and took some back with him. There was never a shortage of playmates there.

At times I felt like I could stay at the Wolf Club forever. We ate well, we were well cared for, and there were always plenty of fun activities. But after a while I missed John and Pat. I didn't just miss them, I missed my life as a guard dog and interacting with people. It's hard to describe, but I knew there was something more for my life. It was fun at the Woof Club, but there was something missing.

John and Pat eventually returned and life got back to normal. I would jog with Pat in the mornings and many afternoons John would take me in the car with him when he went places. In the evenings when John wasn't working, the three of us went to the park down the street. I made friends with a few dogs down there.

I like my new home. It really is amazing how much better things are since living with John and Pat. I should have been dead at least three times already, but instead I am living in a nice house with wonderful people. It's caused me to think more about others, Mom. I see a lot of people on the streets, and part of me wants to do more.

Chapter 17

Come See

One hot summer day in the middle of my afternoon nap, I awoke to the sound of the back patio door opening.

"Come inside and see who's here Daisy." John was standing in the door. I couldn't see anyone else from where I was so I walked towards him. John was always making new friends and often he brought them to the house for a meal, or to just hang out. John liked showing his friends the tricks he taught me. So I went into the house ready for a good game of catch or something.

I entered the back door, but there was no one there.

"Come see who's at the front door Daisy." We walked through the house to the front door and John opened it. Outside I saw a line of boys and girls of all different ages going down our sidewalk and wrapping around the corner. They had old dirty clothes, some were without shoes. They began to enter the house one by one. As each one passed they stopped and greeted me. They all knew my name. Some of them petted me, other leaned over and hugged me. There were dozens of them in the house now.

John said, "Take your new friends out to the patio to play." I ran so fast that I ran right into the sliding glass door. All the children laughed. One of the boys opened the door and in seconds we were all outside.

I showed them all my tricks. They took turns walking me on the leash. We played with every ball and every squeaky toy I had. We played till I was exhausted. Later John set up tables in the patio. Pat brought out sandwiches and drinks for the children. As they sat there eating I counted them. There were almost thirty of them! What were they all doing here?

The children were so hungry. Some of them ate two and three sandwiches. A few kids broke off little pieces of their sandwich and fed me under the table. They were awesome. They had so much energy. When they were outside on the sidewalk, they looked tired and sad, but now they were laughing and talking. They were happy. I had so much fun with the children and lots of sandwiches too. I was so full and tried from playing. I fell asleep under the table while they ate.

When I awoke the table was gone and so were all the children. The afternoon sun was beating down hard on me. I looked around and discovered I was alone in the patio. I was in the same place I laid down hours ago for my afternoon nap. It was all a dream, a wonderful dream.

Chapter 18

The Walls Are Closing In

Dear Mom,

It's been over two years now since we moved to Hermosillo, but my owners have been talking about moving again. It is part of their work. I don't know a lot of the details yet. I don't think we're going back to Santa Rosalia. They keep talking about a bigger city. It's called Monterrey, but I don't know where that is. Hopefully I won't have to go back on that boat. I never want to do that again.

My life here has been good. I have enjoyed guarding the fort, as John says. But some days I feel the walls closing in on me. I want to do more. Maybe it's the same reason I left home all those years ago. I wonder what Monterrey will be like. I've grown a lot here in Hermosillo. I could stay here and be content to guard the fort, but I am also feeling adventurous and ready for something new.

Pat has begun packing boxes again, and John is slowly filling the trailer. There seemed to be less urgency in their move this time. They even seemed a little sadder about the move, especially Pat. I'll write again when I know more.

Chapter 19

The Walls Came Down

Dear Mom,

Well I didn't move to Monterrey. I knew something was coming, but I didn't expected this. Remember the awful reoccurring nightmare I shared with you about being attacked by a pack of dogs in front of the animal hospital in Santa Rosalia? Those dreams stopped a couple of years ago. More recently I've had the reoccurring dream about the children coming to my house to spend the day playing with me. In my dream, the children were very sad outside my house, but were happy when we played together.

Three weeks ago John and Pat took me with them to visit an orphanage called House of Hope. I had visited this place once before. This time, they brought all my food, my leash and even a few of my toys. At first I thought maybe I was heading for a few days of fun with my old pals at The Woof Club. Instead they brought me here.

House of Hope has over twenty-five children of all ages. It's a huge place with lots of room to run and play. They get lots of visitors. Many come to help with the children. I think this might be my new home.

John and Pat never moved to Monterrey because they continue to visit me often, sometimes as much as two or three times a week. They packed up the house, but I don't know where they went for sure. They take me for walks when they come. Often we would go down to the river for a swim. It's always hard to watch them pull away in their car without me. I often wonder if it will be the last time I see them.

I'm not sure how long I will be here. I have enjoyed being with the children. Part of me wants to stay here. I like making the children smile. It feels good to be outside the walls of the patio. In these past three weeks I have learned so much from these children. But part of me misses my home with John and Pat.

Chapter 20

I'm Home

Dear Mom,

Well, there is good and bad news and more good news. The good news is I am still surrounded by my new best friends, the twenty-seven children at the orphanage and their caretakers Tomás and Paola and their three children. They are a terrific family. They work so hard to take wonderful care of the children and me. The bad news is I haven't seen John or Pat for almost six months.

I suspected something was up when they visited last. John brought several very large bags of food, and together John and Tomás carried them to the storage room. I spent the day with John and Pat, but Pat was sad. When it came time to leave Pat didn't want to let go of me. She cried and cried.

John said, "She's gonna be fine Pat. She loves it here." Pat slowly rose to her feet, took John's hand and walked to the car. I watched them drive away for the last time. I think of them a lot. Sometimes I dream about our times together. They were such a big part of my life and they will always be in my heart. I found out later that they moved to

Monterrey and live in a small apartment with no space for dogs. I often wonder how they found this place for me, the place of my dreams. Did they have the same dream I had, the one about the children? Maybe they can read minds? Maybe that's what they're doing when they rub our heads, Mom. They're reading our minds.

The other good news is I have a new best friend. His name is Chuy. He is about the same size as me, a little older, and he has long black hair. He's been guarding the orphanage since long before I got here. He was pretty quiet when I first arrived, but he has always been very nice. Once I got settled in, he started showing me around the neighborhood. The orphanage is way outside of the city. There aren't as many houses and each house has a lot of land around it. The roads aren't paved and there are very few cars on the streets. Sometimes we see people riding horses when Chuy and I walk around the neighborhood.

One day while the children were at school, Chuy and I went out for a late morning walk. The weather was cooler, so the mornings were perfect for walking around a desert town. We often took the same route. We would go a few miles zigzagging through our dusty pueblo. We passed other dogs that lived inside their fenced property. Some were friendlier than others. I have gotten to know many of the dogs. On this particular morning, we explored a small street that was new to me. He really liked showing me his town and teaching me things as we walked. Chuy knew all the roads in town. About half way down the narrow dirt lane, we came across a smaller fenced lot. It had one of those chain link fences like at your house, Mom. Inside the fence was a house that looked similar to ours, and to my surprise there were two dogs lying under the porch that morning, just like we used to do. I stopped and starred at what I was seeing. It was like looking back in time. In fact there was even an old pickup truck parked outside just like at our house.

I struggled to see the two dogs under the porch. I gave a small bark to get their attention. Both of their heads popped up. It looked like two female dogs, one old and one my age. As I starred at the scene in front of me I couldn't help but wonder what my life would have looked like had I never walked through our gate all those years ago. That could have been me lying under the porch day after day letting the world pass me by. Sometimes I think I never should have left home. There's a certain safety in that. The world is full of unknowns and some are better left unknown. Some of the roads I travelled were dangerous, and sometimes I got hurt. But I wouldn't trade any of it because it shaped me to become who I am. I have a limp, but I'm happy. I've suffered loss, but those sorrows gave me a greater appreciation for my joy. Through my journey I discovered who I am and I understand my purpose.

For the longest time I sat there looking at that small house thinking about these things. It's good to look back on occasion. It allowed me to see how far we've come. Chuy and I headed back to the orphanage together. Some of the kids had returned home from school already and they ran to us as we entered the gate. I was home.

Chapter 21

Fly Like an Eagle

Dear Mom,

Yesterday morning the children were up early for school as usual. Chuy and I made the rounds and watched them load into the van and head out with Tomás. He had to make two trips every day because they couldn't all fit in the van together. Afterwards I decided to take a morning walk through the neighborhood. Chuy was sleeping in the sun, so I went alone. I had gone by myself before. I was getting to know my way around pretty well. I started a slow jog down our dusty dirt road.

I still can't get over how much garbage the humans throw on the streets. I like walking around town, but all that garbage is kind of sad. On windy days the garbage sometimes blows right by my face. After walking for a while, I began to smell something. Somebody was cooking, and it smelled really good. I followed the smell for another two blocks. At the corner was a little side street I had never been down before; that's where the smell was coming from. I wandered down the side street. I could see three men up ahead inside a gated lot standing around an open fire. They were cooking something. I stood outside the fence with my nose high in the air sniffing the aroma of cooked meat. One of the men reached into the pot, grabbed a bone and tossed it outside the barbed wire fence. It landed right at my feet. Pork ribs! I knew pork ribs. John loved them and I always got the bones.

I thought I hit a gold mine because as soon as I finished, the man tossed me another, and then another. A second man came over to the gate, pulled down on a piece of metal and swung the gate open in my direction. I hesitated until they threw another rib bone inside the fence. By instinct I went for the bone. A few seconds later I heard the gate close behind me.

The men laughed. "She could be a good guard dog," said one of them.

"Maybe," said another, "She's got a bad leg though."

"As long as she's got a good bark."

The man who opened the gate looked down at me and said in a loud voice, "You got a good bark, dog?" I didn't reply. I was more concerned with how I was going to get out.

One of them brought out an old pot filled with fresh water. It was mid-afternoon now and I was thirsty. They finished eating. Two of them got into a small pickup while the other opened the gate. I walked towards the gate knowing this might be my only chance to get out. The car pulled out and as I followed, the man at the gate scooped up a handful of rocks and threw them at me. I turned my head so as to not get hit in the face. When I looked back, the man closed the gate behind him. They drove off leaving me locked inside.

I spent hours walking every inch of that fence looking for an opening. It was barbed wire with corrugated roofing panels woven in between the wires. I even tried digging. There was a small hole near the back corner of the property that looked like another animal had tried to dig their way out. I scratched at it, but like much of Mexico it was all rock under a thin layer of dirt.

As night fell, I knew the children would be worried about me. I was never gone this long. I wondered what Chuy was doing. Maybe he was looking for me? I was scared and tired and grew sadder by the minute. Was this going to be my new home? Would I never get out? I looked up at the near full moon feeling sad for myself. Then I remembered a story John told me.

"You see that moon, Daisy? It has no light of its own, and it can't move by itself. It is only when the sun shines on the moon that it lights up. We are just like that moon, dark and motionless without God's help. God changes our lives from dark to light, and gives us the power to do all things. Remember that, Daisy. Those who hope in the Lord will renew their strength. They will soar on wings like eagles."

That's when it hit me: I could go over the fence! I ran towards the fence, towards an area just left of the gate. There stood an old rusty file cabinet about two feet from the fence, along with some other scrap metal the men had collected. Further down the fence was an empty milk crate. I bit into the crate, dragged it over and put it upside down about two feet in front of the cabinet. I gazed at the make shift ramp I had just built, then took a few steps back and charged towards the fence. I jumped onto the milk crate and pushed off, causing the crate to flip backwards. As I landed on the file cabinet, I gave a second leap. I closed my eyes and thought, "Soar on wings like eagles!"

I cleared the fence only by inches. As I hit the ground, I let out a cry from the pain in my back leg. I landed on my feet, but the impact caused me to lose my balance and tumble over. I quickly jumped to my feet and ran as fast as I could down the dark narrow road. When I got to the end of the road, I saw a light to the right in the far distance. I ran as fast as I could towards the light. As I got closer, I could see it was a car coming down the street. I slowed down to let it pass. It slowly pulled up next to me. It was hard to see because of the headlights shining. As the car came to a stop, I heard the car door open. In that instant the car's interior light lit up. It was the three men and one was getting out of the car. I took off so fast I could hear the dirt and rocks my paws kicked up hitting the side of their car. I was almost beyond his reach when I felt him grab my collar. I collapsed in exhaustion.

At that same moment, out of the night I saw an object pass in front of me. It was another dog. He leapt into the air onto the man holding my collar, with his jaws wide open, clamping down on the man's arm just above the elbow. The man screamed in agony and let go of my collar in an effort to release himself from the dog's grip. As the man fell to his knees, the dog let go and ran towards me. Together we ran away from the car. I looked back to see if we were being chased, but the man gave up. My eye caught a better look at the dog running next to me. It was Chuy.

If it wasn't for Chuy, I never would have escaped. I was tired, hungry and a little sore, but I was so happy to make it home. Turns out Chuy had been looking for me the whole time. I am so grateful he found me.

Chapter 22

My Best Friend

Dear Mom,

I have so much to tell you. It's been so long since my last letter and so much has happened. I am still at the orphanage. I have watched some of these wonderful children grow up and leave. I have seen others come and receive so much love. My new owners have big hearts for these young souls. I haven't heard from John or Pat in a long time. I hope they are ok. I miss them.

I have some very exciting news, Mom! I am a mom too! Yup, almost a year ago I had four pups. Chuy and I were so happy. We had one male and three female pups. In the first two weeks, two of them died, the male and one female. The other two lived with us until they were grown up. Paola named them Graciela and Esperanza. They were great pups. The children loved being with them and watching them grow up. I learned so much about myself and life by being a Mom. I spent a lot of time caring for Graciela and Esperanza. In the beginning it was tiring. There was not much they could do for themselves. I fed them, cleaned them and taught them everything you taught me, Mom. As they got older it was a lot of work for Chuy, teaching them how to survive, how to behave and how to interact with people. Together I think we were good parents for our pups. Of course Paola and Tomás helped a lot.

It was hard to let go of them, but as they got older we hoped they would have good homes of their own. Graciela left first. I will never forget that day. It was one of the hardest things I've ever done. One of the girls who had been at the orphanage for many years, her name is Melanie, met a young man at University and they got married. Melanie asked Tomás if Graciela could come and live with them. Chuy and I were very happy that Graciela had a good home, but it was still very hard for us. I will always remember her pretty blue eyes looking at me through the car window as they drove off.

Not long after Graciela left, farmer Julio from the village was visiting the orphanage. He and his wife often brought fresh vegetables and homemade bread for the children, but this time he was by himself and very sad. He told us that several days ago his sweet wife Carmelita had passed away. Esperanza was by his feet the whole time he was talking. Esperanza was all black like her dad Chuy and had her dad's long hair. She was very pretty. When Julio returned to his truck to leave Esperanza followed him.

Tomás asked Julio, "Do you have a dog Julio"?

"No I haven't had a dog in years," he responded.

They talked a little more, and the three of them decided that Esperanza would go with farmer Julio. Julio was smiling as they drove off. Esperanza looked so happy in the back of his truck.

Chuy and I are grateful that we get to see the pups from time to time. Farmer Julio brings Esperanza with him when he comes, and Melanie visits with Graciela once in a while.

Life at the orphanage is quiet and busy at the same time. It's quiet because of its location. San Pedro is a small village about forty-five minutes outside of Hermosillo, however, with almost thirty children here there is rarely a dull moment. During the days the kids come and go to school in shifts depending on what grade they're in. At night there is a whole other routine. Dinner is always the highlight of the night. It's the only time of day that the kids are all together. This was also a good time for me and Chuy to catch a snack under the dinner tables.

I used to sleep outside with Chuy. Then one night one of the boys was very sick and crying a lot. He asked Paola if I could sleep with him that night. She agreed. The next night he asked again, and again Paola agreed. The following night one of the other boys had an idea. He faked a sore throat and a cough. As he went to bed, he asked Paola if I could sleep with him. After that there were a lot of sore throats and coughs. I slept in a different bed every night, some nights in the boy's dorm and some nights in the girl's dorm. Paola eventually had to make a calendar to keep the children from fighting over who got to sleep with me. I couldn't keep track of it, but they did. Occasionally one of the younger children would wet the bed. One time the young boy blamed me, but Paola knew better.

With the pups gone, Chuy and I have grown very close. We do almost everything together. We get along great, but sometimes we get frustrated with each other. Usually it's over something pretty small. In the end we move on. He has become my best friend, and I can't imagine my life without him. I've lost owners, but I hope I never lose Chuy.

Chapter 23

Visitors

Dear Mom,

It's been three years since I've seen John and Pat. I didn't think I would ever see them again. Then one day last week they came to the orphanage. Pat looked the same, but John got a little fatter. They had a different car. When they first pulled in I didn't recognize them. I thought it was just another visitor coming to help with the children. When John stepped out of the car, I did a double take. Then He called my name.

"Come on Daisy," he said. I knew that voice in an instant. For a second I thought I was dreaming. Then Pat's door opened. I sprang to my feet and ran towards her. I jumped on her as she was climbing out of the car. She fell back into the seat laughing. I jumped right on her lap and began licking her face and neck.

"I missed you so much baby girl," she said as she hugged and kissed me.

For the next few minutes I ran back and forth between the two of them. Pat was so happy she had tears of joy in her eyes. John was grinning from ear to ear. The three of us went inside where they spoke with Tomás and Paola.

Chuy awoke from his nap to see what all the fuss was. He didn't know my owners very well, but he did remember them. You don't see too many gringos out here in San Pedro, so they kind of stuck out. After everyone chatted for a while, Tomás handed John my leash. I knew what that meant. I ran for the car and waited by the door.

We spent the whole day together. We visited many of our usual places. Pat packed a picnic lunch which included some of my favorite canned dog food. I haven't had it in years.

I was having a great day with them, but I wondered if they were here to take me with them. After spending the day with John and Pat, part of me wanted to be with them again and enjoy the things we used to do together. The other part of me knew that my place was with the children, Tomás and Paola, and with Chuy. I worried a bit because I knew it would not be my decision.

Later that night we returned to the orphanage. Chuy was waiting for me. He wondered if I was gone for good and was so relieved when I returned with John and Pat. They stayed up very late talking with Tomás and Paola. I was very tired from our adventurous day together. I lay at Johns feet listening to them talk. I was trying to figure out if I was leaving with them. I heard them talking about Monterrey. Would that be my new home? I heard them talking about me sleeping with the children. My mind went back and forth. Could I really leave this place? I like it here. It was so hard to do, but in my mind I eventually decided I did not want to go with John and Pat. I was hoping that's what they would decide.

It was after midnight when the four of them stood up and began saying their goodbyes. I nudged Chuy to wake him up. Together we stood up and watched the four of them walk towards us. John put his hand on my head and rubbed my face.

"You're a good girl, Daisy. You've been such a blessing to these children. Keep up the good work baby girl."

Pat was crying as she knelt down to hug me. "I love you Daisy," she whispered.

It was hard to watch them drive off. I don't know if I will ever see them again. The next day I was a bit sad. Seeing them brought back so many good memories. Chuy and I ended the day with a long walk around San Pedro. When we got back home the kids were all gathered around the dinner table. One of the girls at the table called my name and motioned for me to come get a piece of hotdog that she was holding in her hand under the table. I trotted over and gobbled it down. After dinner she and I and two other girls curled up on the couch together. 'This is where I belong,' I thought. These boys and girls love me and I love them. I understood that now, and I think John and Pat did too. That night I climbed into Miguel's bed. It was his turn according to the "Daisy Bedtime Calendar" that hung on the refrigerator. That night I fell asleep in Miguel's bed while he rubbed my belly.

Chapter 24

My Gift

Dear Mom,

I miss you. Some days I wonder if you are still alive. I am pretty sure Dad is gone. He was older than you. It's been over ten years since I left home. Sometimes I can hardly remember your face. The humans have pictures and videos to help them remember their loved ones. I've never seen a photo of you or Dad. My memory of you gets dimmer as I get older. This will probably be my last letter, and that makes me sad.

I am still at the orphanage. I have done a good work here, as John would say. I have seen dozens of young boys and girls receive a lot of love and care. Some days are harder than others. Some days are long and hot. Some days I don't want to be surrounded by so many children. Some days I long to be back with John and Pat sleeping the days away on the patio, going for walks, and riding in the air conditioned car. Some days I wonder if I'm making a difference? There are so many children, Mom, not just here at our orphanage. There are dozens of orphanages around our city. Who knows how many there are in Mexico and around the world.

John used to say, "Be faithful in the little things." I think I have done that here at the orphanage. Often it was just being available to the children, even when I didn't feel like being available. I think our creator has given us all a gift. Mine was to be with these children. I love these children. Making them happy has made my life complete. There are many that I may never reach, but I have been faithful with the ones I could.

Tonight I will have dinner with my children. Maybe play outside afterwards, or watch TV with them. Then I will be available for that one child who has waited for almost a month to have me come and sleep with him in his bed tonight. I am very blessed.

I love you forever Mom,

Daisy

Chapter 25

Hermosillo Observer - San Pedro, Mexico

Emergency crews remain on the scene of last night's massive fire in the 600 Block of Blvd. San Jeronimo in San Pedro. Firemen have worked all night to contain the blaze that began sometime around 1:00 AM this morning. Authorities received an emergency call from Tomás Santos at 1:22 AM. Fire crews from Hermosillo were also called in to assist the San Pedro Fire Department. The two crews worked diligently for several hours through the night to get the burning apartment building under control.

Four families lived in the apartment building. All eighteen of the building's inhabitants escaped with only minor injuries including smoke inhalation and bruises. Authorities are still unsure of the cause of the fire, but reported that once it started, high winds in the area caused it to spread quickly.

We spoke with Mr. Santos, the neighbor at a nearby orphanage who called authorities. "We were all fast asleep at the time of the fire. My dog Daisy began barking alongside my bed. As I got out of bed, she continued to bark while leading me out of the house. Once I got outside, I could see the flames from across the street."

San Pedro Volunteer Fire Department responded quickly, but by the time firemen arrived the building was engulfed in flames. "At that point our only concern was search and rescue" said Captain Ortega. "We evacuated three families safely, and thought that was everyone. However, Mr. Santos' dog barked persistently until we followed her to a fourth one room apartment around back on the second floor. That family would never have survived if it weren't for that dog."

The building is a complete loss. Firemen contained the fire from spreading to other nearby homes, including the adjacent orphanage that housed almost thirty children. Two firemen suffered injuries. They were treated at nearby CIMA Hospital in Hermosillo.

Fire Chief Ortega says this is the largest fire in San Pedro in almost 25 years. "It's a miracle that no one died. It would have been so much worse if we had arrived any later. The winds were blowing the flames directly towards that orphanage. Thank God we were alerted in time."

If you would like to donate clothing or household items to the survivors, they are in need of everything. Donations can be left at House of Hope Orphanage. While you are there, be sure to say hello to San Pedro's most recent hero, Daisy.

Daisy

Update: August 2020

Daisy and Chuy continue to enjoy a quiet life ministering to the children in San Pedro, Sonora MX. Pat and John visit her when they can.

Made in the USA
Middletown, DE
23 December 2022